b

The Child's World®

Published in the United States of America by The Child's World®
1980 Lookout Drive • Mankato, MN 56003-1705
800-599-READ • www.childsworld.com

ACKNOWLEDGMENTS
The Child's World®: Mary Berendes, Publishing Director
The Design Lab: Kathleen Petelinsek, Design and Page Production
Literacy Consultants: Cecilia Minden, PhD, and Joanne Meier, PhD

LIBRARY OF CONGRESS
CATALOGING-IN-PUBLICATION DATA
Moncure, Jane Belk.
  My "b" sound box / by Jane Belk Moncure ;
illustrated by Rebecca Thornburgh.
    p. cm. – (Sound box books)
  Summary: "Little b has an adventure with items beginning with
her letter's sound, such as birds, a baby baboon, a ball, a bat,
and a bicycle."—Provided by publisher.
  ISBN 978-1-60253-142-0 (library bound : alk. paper)
  [1. Alphabet.] I. Thornburgh, Rebecca McKillip, ill. II. Title. III.
Series.
  PZ7.M739Myb 2009
  [E]—dc22   2008033157

A NOTE TO PARENTS AND EDUCATORS:

Magic moon machines and five fat frogs are just a few of the fun things you can share with children by reading books with them. Reading aloud helps children in so many ways! It introduces them to new words, motivates them to develop their own reading skills, and expands their attention span and listening abilities. So it's important to find time each day to share a book or two . . . or three!

As you read with young children, you can help develop their understanding of how print works by talking about the parts of the book—the cover, the title, the illustrations, and the words that tell the story. As you read, use your finger to point to each word, modeling a gentle sweep from left to right.

Simple word games help develop important prereading skills, including an understanding of rhyme and alliteration (when words share the same beginning sound, such as "six" and "sand"). Try playing with words from a book you've just shared: "What other words start with the same sound as moon?" "Cat and hat, do those words rhyme?" The possibilities are endless—and so are the rewards!

My "b" Sound Box®

(Blends are included in this book.)

b

WRITTEN BY JANE BELK MONCURE

ILLUSTRATED BY REBECCA THORNBURGH

Little had a box. "I will

find things that begin with my

b sound," she said. "I will

put them into my sound box."

Little put on her bonnet and

went for a walk.

Little found a bird and
a birdbath.

Did she put the bird and the

birdbath in the box? She did.

Little found a bunny.

Did she put the bunny into

the box with the bird and the

birdbath? She did.

Then Little heard a sound.

"Buzzzzzz." It was a bee.

She put the bee into the box,

carefully!

Next, she found a baby baboon

in a tree.

The baby baboon was eating a banana. "I will put you into my box," said Little .

The box was so big she could

hardly carry it.

She found a bicycle with a basket on the back.

She put the box into the basket and rode the bicycle over a big bump!

The baby baboon, the bunny, and the bird bounced out of the box.

And Little bounced off the

bicycle. "That was a bad bump!"

she said.

Then she saw a ball and a bat.

"Let's play ball!" she said. And

they did.

The baby baboon hit the ball with the bat. The ball bounced into a bush.

Something was behind the bush.

It was a bear. He gave the ball

to Little . "Thank you, Bear,"

she said.

She put the bear, the bush, and

the ball into the box. She put the

baby baboon, the bat, the bird,

the birdbath, and the bunny

back, too.

The bee said, "Buzz, buzz, this

box might break!"

"I must find something

bigger," said Little .

She rode her bicycle over a bridge.

Under the bridge, she saw a boat, a big, big boat.

She jumped into the boat and

took the things out of her box.

"This is big enough," she said.

"Big enough for all

of us." And it was!

Little 's Word List

baboon

ball

banana

basket

bat

bear

bee

bicycle

bird

birdbath

boat

bonnet

box

bridge

bump

bunny

bush

Other Words with Little

bag

balloon

barn

basketball

bathtub

bed

bell

belt

bone

book

bottle

bowl

brush

bug

butterfly

More to Do!

Little had quite an adventure when she put on her bonnet! You can play a fun game with things that begin with the letter b.

Directions:

Begin by sitting in a circle with your friends. Have one person hold a small ball. This person is the first player. The first player says:

I was on my bike.
Then I hit a bump...
A big, big bump!
And into my basket bounced a _____.

(Here the player names something that starts with a b sound.)

The first player now passes the ball to the person sitting to the right. The new player repeats the rhyme. He or she must include the **b** object the first player said and add a new **b** object. Each player repeats the rhyme, naming all the things that have been said and adding one more. See how long you can keep the game going!

Here are a few words to get you started:

backpack	bead	biscuit	bowl
badger	bean	bobcat	bracelet
banjo	berry	boot	button

About the Author

Best-selling author Jane Belk Moncure has written over 300 books throughout her teaching and writing career. After earning a Master's degree in Early Childhood Education from Columbia University, she became one of the pioneers in that field. In 1956, she helped form the Virginia Association for Early Childhood Education, which established the first statewide standards for teachers of young children.

Inspired by her work in the classroom, Mrs. Moncure's books have become standards in primary education, and her name is recognized across the country. Her success is reflected not only in her books' popularity with parents, children, and educators, but also by numerous awards, including the 1984 C. S. Lewis Gold Medal Award.

About the Illustrator

Rebecca Thornburgh lives in a pleasantly spooky old house in Philadelphia. If she's not at her drawing table, she's reading—or singing with her band, called Reckless Amateurs. Rebecca has one husband, two daughters, and two silly dogs.